LAND of the PAW PAW

A Canadian fairy tale with scientific meaning.

About a fabulous and delicious tropical fruit made up of sweet custard that is able to grow in a snowy winter.

About a fantastic robot who disliked exploitation.

About a botanist creating a good fairy tale in the world.

There is one big island in the tropics. There, the big yellow sun pours warm light everywhere, giving life to all the plants. The energy of life fills the island and weakens the gravity. Everyone feels very light, and bold water droplets float away and play with the light. The sun's rays pierce the water molecules, and a rainbow appears in the sky! Heavy drops of water flow down all the coloured arcs of the rainbow and they water every small sprout reaching for the sun. For eternity, not even a single small twig was left without attention. This beautiful place is called Cuba.

A small Paw Paw twig lived here. Lived and rejoiced. Not needing any money. So she thought, "I wish everyone could live peacefully and happily like this." That's how kind and cheerful this Paw Paw twig is!

And by an incredible coincidence, just as the answer to the question "why" is always "lucky"

In Cuba, a scientist appeared next to the Paw Paw twig. He was looking for traces of tropical plants that would lead to the north. He wanted to follow their footsteps and dreamed of finding a sprout of such a tree that could make wonderful tropical fruits in cold weather. He really wanted to start growing beautiful, juicy fruits in his native northern country of Canada. He started talking about it, and his friend the wind carried the words of the old botanist sitting under a palm tree to the Paw Paw twig.

She heard him say,

"I have an old dream, because of which I became a botanist. I wished that tropical fruits could grow in Canada and give their amazing fruits to all the children living there. All my life, I've wanted to find at least one tropical plant that could put its roots down into cold soil."

The botanist jumped up in surprise. As if by magic, right next to him, the Paw Paw Twig had appeared. She was a fabulous girl in a green dress. A drawing of a plant with green leaves stretched across her entire dress. She had a burgundy flower in her hair.

She said to him,

"Look what I can do" (the magical twig smoothly moved her hand to the side and behind her back and pulled out a big green and yellow fruit shaped like a potato which had a beautiful soft yellow custard inside).

Then she said,

"I can make fruits like these, and I like the cold weather and snow. Maybe everyone in Canada will like me. I am a tropical fruit that can survive the cold winters. I will grow up and give wonderful fruits like these to everyone in Canada. What do you think? Will I be able to become that tropical fruit tree that you want for everyone in Canada?”

The scientist was surprised by the appearance of this magical girl, and he answered her briefly in a non-scientific way,

“I think that your fruits are exactly what we need. What do you want in return for giving your amazing fruits away?”

She hadn't thought about getting something in return for her kindness before. She listened intently to the botanist. From her hair, a brown flower almost fell on the old man's nose.

The magical girl came up with what she wanted in return and exclaimed,

“I want to hear "Thank you!" as often as possible!”

Pollen from the brown flower got into the old man's nose.

He sneezed and said,

"So it will be! For me, sneezing symbolizes good luck!”

The old man was a very experienced botanist. All his experience with plants had turned into intuition, so he knew that the girl was being honest about her intent.

The botanist lived in Cuba and was friends with the local trees. Sometimes when he wanted tender coconut pulp he just stretched out his hand. A palm tree immediately threw a cracked open coconut into the palm of his hand.

The same coconut palm said,

“You can't leave! You're the best coconut soccer player in all of Cuba. I will let you leave if you can guess what the fruit that my friend will give you is”

Then a neighboring green bush gave him a piece of pineapple. The scientist put it on his tongue and enjoyed how the juice flowed into his mouth. Nature’s work is so fabulous. The rich, fruity taste of the tropical jungle pleasantly excited his appetite.

The palm tree was waiting for an answer, and the botanist said,

"I'm sorry, I didn't recognize this fruit."

The botanist turned to the Paw Paw twig and said,

“Dear Paw Paw Twig, do you know that the country of Canada is very far up north? I'm so old that I don't have the strength to go on this adventure. You can't get there alone. And even if you get there, tropical fruits don't usually grow there. I'm needed here myself. I have to guess the names of different fruits that everyone brings me everyday.”

He yawned and said,

“Such hard work”

The twig did not give up and said,

“I have a friend, who knows everything and has seen everything. He will tell me how to get to where I want to go. And then, in Canada, the botanists living there will help me with finding a good piece of land to call home. Then, fruits will appear on my branches.”

The botanist answered,

“Okay, I see that you're as persistent and stubborn as the local barbados cherry. I'll help you. I know how to reach the person that your talking about. He loves trees and has hugged them and helped them grow since his childhood. He has become a monopolist of the flat tasteless raspberries that grow in Canada. That is why he is called "the raspberriesboy". He knows a lot about botany, I'll ask him to come and help you with the move."

This raspberriesboy that they had talked about finally arrived in the tropics less than a hundred years after this. Only his name was also the Monopolist of flat tasteless raspberries. He looked at the Paw Paw twig, and he liked her.

Then she asked him,

"Is there at least one small place for me in your Canadian village?"

"I've already found one place for you. That's why I came to pick you up. This spot is just not good without you. You will decorate it with your Kind. It will become the most beautiful place in the world"

The magic twig stood and swung her hands like paint brushes, drawing something in the air. With the tips of her fingers, she spread her hands from one point to another, and then brought them together again, creating a cluster of fruits hanging from one of her hands.

The boy praised her,

“You can make very good fruits"

"Thank-You-Very-Much!", the Paw Paw twig sang.

They did not waste any time, and on the same day they decided to hit the road. They came to say goodbye to all sorts of fruits. The raspberriesboy had never even heard of such fruits. Here was a plant with fruit in the form of round green pinecones that came up and said to the raspberriesboy,

“Our name is Cherimoya. We are relatives of the Paw Paw. If you need to know our genetics or our soil needs, then contact us. We are called “the ice cream fruit”.

"You're the best!" the raspberriesboy exclaimed.

He loved ice cream very much.

The Annona fruit tree proclaimed loudly and confidently,

"I am the best, the most delicious fruit in the tropics is a sugar apple from my tree."

“We'll see about that when I grow up. We don't argue about our tastes"

Said the Paw Paw twig, she had a healthy and correct opinion about everyone.

The Cherimoya said to the raspberriesboy,

“The Paw Paw’s exotic taste glorifies itself. We are more worried about her health and if she can grow in such a cold place.”

The raspberriesboy answered,

“Don't worry too much about her health. I'm a doctor for trees. You can call me the Tree Doctor. With my care, even ginseng can grow well. It is the hardest plant to grow, ginseng the miracle plant"

And it was time for them to go on their journey. And so, the raspberriesboy said,

"Let's go!"

And of course, they did not actually go, but they swam to North America on a big ship. Again, you would be wrong. As it turned out, you would be wrong to say "to swim" on a ship. It would be correct to say "to travel". That's how difficult everything is in life. And you don't want to, but you ask: "Why?" In response, you will hear "good for you"

***

Isn't it long, isn't it short, but their large ship arrived on the southern coast of America. On the shore, the travelers saw a road headed North.

The Paw Paw twig asked,

"Are there a lot of roads going North, or just one?"

The raspberriesboy answered her,

“There are a lot. North America is a civilized place and there are roads everywhere. Their information system has developed up to computers and the internet. I'll turn on an internet navigator that will lead us to Canada."

The travelers started walking to Canada. They went and saw place along the road without a single plant. The fairy tale Twig wanted to plant something on one of these empty places.

She said,

“I'm not a magic wand. To live my life is not as easy as aimlessly crossing a field. I need to do good with my own hands"

The Paw Paw Twig stood in the middle of the lot. She put her hand on the ground and magic happened. Where her hand had touched the ground, a small Paw Paw seedling appeared. It swayed with the wind, dancing.

“I suppose that he likes it here, it means that this is a good place for him to grow up in!”,

the fairy-tale girl rejoiced.

The travelers heading towards Canada saw Mr Lemon driving by in a big car. He stopped next to the travelers. He did not offer to offer the hitchhikers a ride, but only said,

“This is my road.”

Travelers looked around and saw a sign that said "my road".

“My road goes to the south underwater, until it reaches Cuba. Then again under water until it reaches South America. Then through South America and underwater until it reaches Antarctica. Many more trees need to be cut down so that I can extend my beautiful road”

"Good for you," the boy replied, trying to be polite. He then turned to the Paw Paw twig and, unbothered by

Mr Lemon, twirled his finger around on his temple and said,

“He's crazy. The earth belongs to everyone. You've just appeared here, and this road belongs to you, and to everyone else on this planet.”

The Paw Paw twig liked the words of the fabulous botanist and said,

“I also think that water, air, and earth belong to everyone. It's not necessary to take anything away from those who were born earlier than you and “own” everything. There is no need to fight each other. We need to grow up and live together and share the beautiful earth that we live on with each other.”

Shouting "My road!" Mr Lemon raced ahead of them in a car.

The fairy-tale girl put her palm to the ground. Another small sprout came out of the ground. He released two green leaves and swayed with the wind.

The two friends went along the road past an orange grove. Everyone was eating oranges. Children were biting off bright slices of fruit. The scent of orange zest had made its way to the travelers. Life had become more fun. The fabulous raspberriesboy and the Paw Paw twig walked through the neatly planted trees. Someone's magic hands had planted an orange grove before them.

They went far past the grove. They got to a place where Mr Lemon had assigned high prices to all the fruits. There, people had no money to buy oranges from him at his high prices.

Mr Lemon has to do a lot to make the prices so high. Most of the oranges are taken and crushed by tractors to keep the price high for the remaining oranges.

At one point, when they were walking down the orange grove from before, such a tractor growled sharply. It pressed a heavy metal scoop on a pile of oranges. The fruits got crushed on a flat surface, but some were still able to escape.

Then the Paw Paw twig saw five oranges rolling away in a hurry. They rolled along the smooth surface of fruits. They were looking for a hole to hide in. They found a hole and immediately fell into it. The shelter they found did not save them. In one second, a sharp crack was heard, the tractor had run over the oranges, and it had crushed them.

They buried the living vitamins into the ground. The Paw Paw twig was sad to see the gifts of nature being wasted. They hid fruits from those ordinary people who are busy working for the gain of other people. These same people don't have enough money to buy food at the high prices that Mr Lemon is charging.

Back on the road, they ran into an obstacle. A meter above the ground, across the whole road, a long metal rod was put up. Mr Lemon was standing at the barrier selling lemonade. Next to him, the Paw Paw twig appeared and said,

“There is something bad happening right now, juicy and sweet oranges are being wasted”

"How are you allowing this to happen?", the monopolist of flat tasteless raspberries added.

Mr Lemon dodged their question and said,

“That's stupid. I came up with the idea of blocking the road with a barrier and stopping people from going any further so that they would buy lemonade from me and not ask any nonsense questions.”

A hard-working person came and bought a glass of lemonade so he could continue going on the road, as he had no other option. As soon as the person left, Mr Lemon opened the tap on the sewage pipe hanging from above the lemonade container. He added water to the jar of lemonade.

The raspberries boy was mad and said,

“Why are you diluting your lemonade with sewage water?”

Mr Lemon answered,

“Wait a minute, I shouldn’t do this in front of other people! I myself will not dilute my lemonade in front of everyone, and I will tell my tractor drivers not to crush oranges when passers-by see. Thanks for the clever advice!”

The Paw Paw Twig shook off the brown flower on her hair and gave him an answer,

“We will not buy any lemonade from you. You're very bad. You should go think about something good and maybe even do something good!”

The friends walked around the barrier and walked on. Behind themselves, they heard Mr Lemon yell,

"I dream of getting a yacht, to walk around and guard my road."

This time, the Paw Paw twig twirled her finger at her temple before answering,

“First, you would need to grow legs on your yacht or put wheels on it for it to travel down the road. Now, I understand that he is so crazy. In his head, he lives in his one road, and he won’t go anywhere else except for it.”

The wind-friend blew into their back. The wind was their friend. It helped them as much as it could, it pushed them on their way up north. It helped them so much throughout their journey.

The wind spoke to the Paw Paw twig,

“Your fruits are very fragrant, but I don't know how I can eat them since I have no hands or a mouth, but I want them to grow everywhere, so that wherever I go, I will always sense the delightful smell of the paw paw fruits. Do you know that the smell is made up of tiny pieces of the fruit!”

The Paw Paw twig asked,

“Where are you going, wind?”

He answered,

“I am going to where I'm wanted”

The Paw Paw twig asked the wind,

“Am I wanted somewhere?”

The Wind answered,

“Everyone is wanted somewhere; it is your job to go and find where you are wanted”.

The wind shared his wisdom and flew away. He probably forgot to wind up a windmill somewhere.

The friends walked by some apple orchards. The beauty of the apple trees is indescribable. The apple tree's spirit enveloped both of them in a pleasant atmosphere. And like before, they kept on going forward. But not further than a big fire in the middle of the road. A woman named Madame Viperis with a tangled mess of hair on her head stood at the fire. She was breaking off branches from the apple trees and throwing them into the fire. The fire was burning everything.

This is all a big dirty trick that Madame Viperis pulling. She has to take apples from the apple trees as a fine. It turns out she takes branches from the whole orchard, as punishment for a single trees wrongdoing, she punishes all the trees. For the actions of an individual, the entire population is punished. She puts the branches on the fire to be burnt. The raspberries boy and the Paw Paw twig thought she would take the apples that she takes and give them out for everyone to eat. And what happened. Some characters live in the chaos of evil and everything that they do turns into evil. There is nothing standing in between the world of good and the chaos of evil. Only people themselves somehow get from one to another. Here she is, Madame Viperis, who will shortchange for the apple collection, how and how much money everyone should pay fines. She will figure it out and punish anyone.

She had decided to replace fines with punishments. But these are not the same thing. What if a tree has no apples left, she can cut branches off? She cuts the tree's branches off as a punishment, killing the apple tree. She torments the trees with her own hands without any remorse. Such insensitive people like her are called sociopaths.

She walked up to travelers and said,

“Pay the fine, young people.”

There were people in uniforms with weapons standing around them. The situation became very scary, and because of this, and her request sounded more like a punishment. The travelers were scared.

"We don't have any apples to give to you," the raspberries boy answered.

Madame Viperis said to him,

“I have to take a fine from everyone. If you don't have any apple, I'll take that small twig!”

She grabbed the Paw Paw twig. She tried pulling Paw Paw twig, wanting to throw her into the fire, and said,

“If you can't give me an apple, I'll throw the twig into the fire!”

The Paw Paw pulled itself out from her grasp in the opposite direction. She tried to get out.

The raspberriesboy stood up for her. He pulled the magical girl towards him and pulled her out of the tenacious paws of the villainess.

He said,

“You can't burn the Paw Paw twig! She will bring joy to everyone in Canada and the USA"

A girl Manager came in a T-shirt with the inscription "oink".

Madame Viperis began to read aloud column of the words "Oink".

The girl Manager asked Madame Viperis,

“Stop oink please. Here's a money, I will pay for the travelers.”

Having gotten a fine, Madame Viperis left the travelers alone.

The Paw Paw Twig ran off to the side. She then put her hand on the ground. A small sprout came out of the ground. The sprout put out two fresh green leaves.

Their friend, the wind, blew on the sprout lightly, and it swayed with each small gust. The Paw Paw waved goodbye to him. Then the twig ran up to catch up to her friends.

The raspberriesboy asked the girl Manager that had helped them out,

“Thanks for your help. Let’s talk?”

She answered him,

"My name is Califoria, I am able to help you because I have money. I came up with the idea of pansion, and now I have a lot of money."

The raspberriesboy asked her,

"What is this?

"A boarding house is when people do work for me so that they can live in my boarding houses or hotels. If you want to live there, do work for me."

The Paw Paw Twig said to her,

"That is not good, people shouldn't live only to work. I should work to live just sometimes. Sometimes I drink water to live, for example. I don't live to drink water"

Califoria said to her,

"That doesn't matter."

"My life is not "That doesn't matter""

"Nobody demands money from you for water!? It's probably because you're made of wood."

They did not notice that they had reached a huge camp full of tents.

The girl said,

“This is one of my boarding camps”

She was happy to offer help to the travelers, “You can stay here, I won't take anything from you. Just have to work for me everyday”

In front of their eyes, Mr Lemon was cutting through a forest of giant sequoia trees.

Mr Lemon said to her,

“If you give me some more money California, I'll cut down all the forests in America for you to build more tent cities.”

They all reached the big garbage dump in the middle of the camp together. A robot was sorting trash with his five hands. He is very agile with his five hands. For this they called him, Patieruke . Quickly, he put one thing from one place to another.

He saw the group of people and complained to them,

“The girl-manager Califoria promised to work and collaborate with me and called me a "cobot". Which means a collaborative robot. But she doesn't collaborate with me or help me with anything.”

The girl said to the group,

“This robot is such a fool. He believed all my promises. People help me because of my intentions but in the end receive nothing from me. Do you understand that Cobot?”

The girl-manager was a very good communicator. She looked at the talking piece of metal with a smile. However, even the robot's eye did not believe her hypocritical smile.

The robot said to her,

“I'm offended, you're an evil and manipulative person, I'm leaving!”

Suddenly, the Paw Paw twig appeared next to the robot.

The Paw Paw twig said to him,

“I don't know who you are, but I see that you're making the right choice. In your life, you should decide where you should go and what you should do. You are good person. You can trust my promises.”

“I am Patieruke . My hand is a rifle, and a neon light is on inside of me”,

the cobot found with whom he wants to cooperate and decided to leave the manager's girl.

“I'll leave you California. You don't try to fix robots. You're only exploiting me for profit. I'll fall apart here with you, but I still have to save humanity, or my help will come in handy for a magical girl. Take me with you Pow Pow. I'll be nice to you.”

The Paw Paw twig said,

“Come with us cobot. Life is more fun when you are with others"

The Twig leaned towards the Cobot and said something to him very quietly,

"I want to leave unnoticed; will you help me leave without saying goodbye to the girl that runs this boarding city. I don't want to say goodbye to the girl and to Mr Lemon. Call me discreetly. I'll pretend to be talking to someone.”

Patieruke came up to California and said,

“All of your precious money has lost its value by 1000 times in recent years. In fact, zeros mean nothing now. I hope that it loses its value even more, goodbye.”

California frowned and said to him,

“Don't worry about me. I have gotten 1000 times more money in recent years, goodbye calculator”

The phone at the Paw Paw twig rang. That's where the trick comes from. Business Paw Paw twig spoke on the phone.

While all of this was happening, the raspberriesboy and the Paw Paw twig quietly walked away. The whole group of friends went on their own way up north.

The Paw Paw twig remembered the words of the old botanist about how he was looking for traces of tropical plants. She did not forget to leave her mark in every place that she visited. She put her hand on the ground and a small sprout came out of the ground. He shot out two green leaves like the others before him. The new Paw Paw sprout stood up and swayed, dancing. The Paw Paw twig smiled. It's very nice of her to leave green seedlings everywhere.

And so, they headed further on their journey to Canada.

After walking further for a long time. The Paw Paw twig looked around and saw the great Niagara Falls. She then looked at the lake on the left, then at a lake in front of her, then at a lake on the right. She rearranged the first letters of the names of the lakes, Huron, Ontario, Michigan and Erie. She got the word "home". She looked at the beautiful place and said,

“This is an amazing place with a lot of water, enough for all the plants to share. I'm going to stay here and call this place my home!”

The raspberriesboy said,

“This place is called tomato country; this is my home. Look at how tomatoes still ripen in November, I think that here you will still have enough time to ripen your fruits in the fall.”

She then asked the tomato plants,

“Would you tomatoes be kind enough to share a bit of land with me the Paw Paw?”

The raspberriesboy said,

“Don't worry, everyone here likes to work together and help each other. Follow me, I think that I know a perfect place where a lot of plants are growing well, and there we'll find some land for you. We will visit each other. Let's go visit me now and find the land for you.”

“We did not have time to appear and immediately visit”, Patieruke spread all five hands in surprise.

Down on the lake, the Paw Paw twig saw the fishermen. They pulled fish out of the water with baskets.

The Paw Paw twig exclaimed,

"Fish, I love this place so much!”

The wind friend blew in back, urging the curiosity of the Paw Paw twig.

“Go forward to adventure Paw Paw twig”, said the wind friend.

The magical girl has the power of curiosity like the wind friend. This force pulls her forward to meet with adventure.

***

The Paw Paw twig and the raspberriesboy arrived in a forest clearing with rays of sunlight beaming down on all the plants growing there.

The Paw Paw twig stopped in the middle of the clearing and stretched both arms up into the sunlight. The sun filled the little sorceress with light. A sprout appeared in the luminous hands of the Paw Paw twig, and she planted it in the soil. The sprout developed roots, and those roots dug through the rich black soil until they found water. So she planted more and more Paw Paw seedlings around. Then the fairy-tale girl gathered sunlight in her palms and sprinkled it on the grown tree. The tree grew flowers like the brown flower in her hair. Then the flowers began to turn into fruit. Soon, Paw Paw fruits grew in the crown of huge green leaves on the new tree.

The raspberriesboy saw a cluster of fruit and asked the Paw Paw twig to share her fruits with everyone who came.

The raspberriesboy gathered a large group of guests in the unusual garden. There were beautiful Paw Paw trees all around with large leaves that created a shady place for everyone to sit down. The raspberriesboy said,

“I will treat everyone with different roots, berries, and fruits, aside from being tasty they have flavonoids and vitamins! That means basic treats on the table.”

A squirrel with a puffy black fur coat yawned, stretched his arms upwards and said,

“I can't relax, I want candy!!”

The Paw Paw twig said to the raspberriesboy,

“Give him a sweet carrot or a sweet Jerusalem artichoke. Let him eat and enjoy every bite. Everything in nature is perfect. Since his birth, nature has given him everything he needs for life, air, tasty food, and even a dark night, so he can sleep quietly. No one should dare to stop people from being able to have these things!”

A green bush with a lot of big white flowers everywhere on his branches walked into the circle of friends. This is the clumsy Cordial Dale the elderberry plant, who leaned over and showed off all his white flowers and said,

“Who came up with the idea of giving everyone here a tasty treat? I can make some tasty treats for everyone as well. Here's a sweet, sugary drink called elder flower cordial that I can make from my flowers!”

A small green stick fell out from underneath one of Cordial Dales leaves. It suddenly jumped on the Paw Paw tree's bark. Looking closely, you could see a small triangular head and two spiky green claws, the green praying mantis immediately drew attention to himself, and then he said,

“I like healthier things, fruits that have just begun to ripen always have more vitamins than the completely ripe ones”

He saw a Paw Paw fruit on the bottom of the cluster with a small yellow spot of ripeness, the Praying Mantis asked her,

“Paw Paw, could you please give me the fruit with the yellow solar imprint?”

The Paw Paw gave it to him, and then he said,

“Perfect, it is not completely ripe, so it should have a lot of vitamins, thanks!”

“You're welcome”

Said the Paw Paw.

After the Mantis being so kind, she began to treat the guests with affection.

A squirrel asked her,

“Paw Paw, could I also treat myself to a tropical custard fruit?”

“Yes, take this fruit”,

Answered the Paw Paw tree.

“Could you please give me some fruit with the taste of the tropics?”

Asked someone else.

“Yes, here you go, enjoy my tropical delight!”

Answered the Paw Paw tree.

And the Paw Paw Tree did not notice how it had begun to give away fruits that were completely green. When everyone tried them, they were hard, bitter and inedible.

Everyone that came to visit thought that the tree was joking with them.

“What kind of wooden bananas are these? Are they for beauty as a decoration to put in a shop window. Right?”,

asked Cordial Dale.

“He can cut them”

“All palm trees grow and sing bananas, and our Paw Paw has wooden fruits that are green to the touch”

After the rumors of the “wooden fruits” spread around the forests, a pesky wood eating Weevil came to the Paw Paw tree and drilled a hole into the fruit and tried to eat the inside, hoping that it was wooden.

Even he said,

“Oh, look here inside the seeds!”

The Paw Paw girl was very upset by all of this humor and did not want to give any fruits to anyone.

The raspberriesboy said,

“Keep your fruits on the tree until New Years. Let them mature. I will make sweets from part of yours fruits. We will make New Year's gifts for children with them. We will also hang tropical candies on the branches. We will serve them for the New Year feast that we have in our forest. And then we don’t have enough carrots for sweets for everyone. You will happy New Years tree. Are you agree?”

The Paw Paw happily replied,

"I agree"

She does not know how to be angry for a long time. She is good and the world of goodness around her turns into a good fairy tale.

Finally, when the time had come for the New Year feast. All the Paw Paws fruits had become yellow completely, and they dropped to the ground because of their ripeness. When the raspberriesboy came, he was amazed by the sweet tropical smell.

Under the waltzing snowflakes, the fairy-tale girl Paw Paw waved her hands as if she were painting. And as if by magic, various treats appeared on a big table in the forest clearing. Everyone gathered in the clearing and sat down at the table.

The Paw Paw twig pointed to the big pile of soft and aromatic, yellow Paw Paw fruits in the middle of the table and said,

“Everything is as right as the raspberriesboy loves.”

The fairy-tale girl Paw Paw, with a smooth movement of her hand, pointed to a pile of fruit candies. They were wrapped in white glitter wrappers. Their shape was curved to resemble the shape of Paw Paw fruit.

“Can I treat everyone with these tropical delights?”

"You sure can",

the company replied cheerfully, ready to give her a second chance. That’s how the forest's inhabitants live, they share everything with one another and forgive each other for previous mistakes and always give each other a second chance.

The guests tried the soft, scrumptious fruits. All the fruit candies from the huge pile had disappeared without a trace. There is no better compliment for taste. Everyone ate it without a trace, this meant that it was delicious. And all the guests gave a big "Thank you!" to the Paw Paw Twig and walked away with a wide smile on their faces, which of course were covered with fruit custard from the Paw Paw fruits. Seeing how everyone was so happy because of the delicious fruits, the raspberriesboy said,

"Paw Paw twig, your dream has come true! Everyone has given you a "Thank you very much!" for what you have done. As a result of what you have done, our garden city has blossomed with an unusual type of flower, smiles!”

The Paw Paw twig became an irreplaceable friend, making the lives for everyone of those around her full of kindness. Her magical fruit, giving everyone who tasted it, a peek into a tropical fairy tale. And this is the actually fairy tale.

Here this fairy tale ends,

While the Paw Paw trees journey has only begun.

And to those who have listened attentively, well done!

Rainy day (by J Vasilyev)

Oh, rainy day, take me far, far away.

To a place with sun where I can play.

Where I'll love it so much, I'll want to stay.

No more clouds and gloomy days

A place where there is only light

A place where it's quiet at night.

No thunder no storms.

A place that does not fit the norms.

I think I've found this place
And it is here to state its case
Here's what it said
This place is home, in your bed
You'll enter it when you close your eyes and fall asleep
And when you will fall down very deep
Into the kingdom of your sleep.

*Illustrations by Jonathan Vasilyev

www.ingramcontent.com/pod-product-compliance
Lightning Source LLC
Chambersburg PA
CBHW042054110726
48006CB00002B/394
9798838762115